I0788385

This book is dedicated to the individuals who provide and hold
a safe space for children to develop, Learn, play and enjoy stories.

Dear Storyteller,

"Amir's Brave Adventure" is a story designed to help children overcome fear and anxiety while learning about trust, mindfulness, and connection. The story is based on Dr. Janet Courtney's FirstPlay® Kinesthetic Storytelling® method also known as "BACK Stories". Kinesthetic Storytelling® is a multi-sensory attachment focused therapeutic approach that incorporates interactive touch activities with metaphoric and imaginative storytelling.

Since completing Dr. Janet Courtney's FirstPlay® Kinesthetic Storytelling® training I have utilize "The Magic Rainbow Hug" within the playroom with children with Autism Spectrum Disorder, sessions with children and parents focused on attachment, sensory, play and storytelling. Developing and maintaining a story telling routine, with touch based activities can increase the social, attachment and engagement skills of children. Amir's journey has the ability to reach multiple issues within various environments.

This story was written to assist children to identify and name symptoms of anxiety, to embrace differences, face fears and learn mindfulness techniques.

This story also has a focus on the adult and child relationship, to help the adult create a space for positive and creative bonding. I have utilized Amir's story alongside adoptive parents creating new spaces with children who present with trauma and issues with attachment. Being present for the transformation and increased bonding between the family will always be in my heart.

The story is of Amir, a leopard cub who is different from the other cubs and worries that he does not fit in. He has a lot of fears. His fears prevent him from earning his leopard spots. It's not until his friend Zola encourages him to trust her and venture out of his comfort zone to be brave and face his fears that he starts the journey of overcoming fear and anxiety.

This book provides multi-sensory elements such as imagination, touch, sound, visual and mindfulness that allows children to hear and feel Amir's journey.The elements offer an opportunity to increase adult and child attachment.

Per Dr. Courtney, research touch can help reduce stress in children. When a child receives safe and caring touch, the feel-good "love" hormone oxytocin is released the stress hormone, cortisol is decreased

This book includes additional information and activities focused on:
friendship, identifying anxiety, developing coping skills, building confidence, mindfulness and being brave. There are many possibilities with this story and my goal is for children to have a safe and playful experience.

Thank you, Storytellers,
Carmen Jimenez-Pride

How to Use This Book

An illustrated children's story is created to engage the child's imagination. This book has the benefit of being read as a traditional story or as an interactive story to read and do the touch based activated on the child's back.

Ask the child if they feel comfortable sitting in front of you so you can have access to their back, you want to make sure you have room to complete the hand movements on the child's full back. The BACK Stories technique is not a massage technique and is done with the clothes on.

Prior to starting you want to assure you, as the caregiver is calm, relaxed and present. You want to create a nurturing space for the child with positive energy.

When incorporating touch, always ask children for permission to draw the story on their back. If the child is not ready for the BACK story you can offer to draw on their hands.

All of the hand movements can be found at the bottom of the page.
A detailed glossary of hand movements can be found at the end of the story.
Remember this is a starting point make the movements yours.

Let's go on an adventure with Amir

The sun was shining bright and the sky was blue with fluffy white clouds over the rainforest. The Leopard cubs were flowing with the waterfall and swimming in the blue lake.

The cubs were **running** and **jumping** from tree to tree. The Leopard cubs were **happy** and laughing.

Amir was watching the cubs **run** and play but did not join them. He did not look like the other cubs. Amir was golden in color, but he did not have any **spots**.
This made Amir very sad. He felt like he was different, he did not want to play with the other cubs.

ir did not feel brave and had many fears. He did not feel strong or art, and he did not want to try new things. Amir felt like the other Leopard cubs did not like him.

brave

Amir's mother was beautiful and golden with many spots. His father was black with black spots and they called him a Black Panther! "Amir when you face your fears you will earn your spots." Said mom and dad. They encouraged him to go out and be brave.

Amir's friend, Zola, one of the leopard cubs, would always ask him to come play. Each time Amir would say "NOOOOOO", in a scared voice.

When Amir thought about going to play with the other cubs
he would sometimes feel:
His heart beating fast.
He had trouble breathing.
Feelings of wanting to hide.
Feeling like he could not move.
heart beating
breathing

One day Amir's friend Zola begged and begged Amir to come and play. Zola smiled really big and danced around and said, "Amir I will help you face your fears and earn your spots"
spots

Listening to Zola's playful and caring voice and looking at her bright smile, Amir had feelings of trust. He felt safe. He felt confident. Amir stood tall and decided to face his fears and trust Zola.

Amir and Zola **ran** fast through the tall **grass** in the rainforest. To his surprise he noticed a **spot** on his paw, so he ran faster and noticed more spots on his paws.

They were **jumping** in the **lake** and diving into the **waterfall**. Zola exclaimed, "Amir, WOW look at your **spots**!"
He looked and smiled, and they continued to play in the water.
Amir felt strong.

They came to a large tree. Zola ran up the tree but Amir stopped. Zola said, "Come on Amir, you can see so many beautiful things from up here."
Amir felt sad, he began to feel his heart beat fast and felt like he could not move. He said in a low voice, "I'm scared it's a really tall tree."

Zola climbed down the tree and said with a soft voice, "Amir, look at
all your spots, you have faced so many fears today."
Let's try something I do when I feel scared. Do you want to try it?
Amir said "yes."
Zola continued and said, "do what I do;"
Stand tall and proud, feet firm on the ground.
Close your eyes, if you feel comfortable, and take a deep breath. In
through your nose filling your tummy and out through your nose
letting all the air out of your tummy.
Zola said, "repeat after me; I am calm, I am confident, and
I am brave."

When Amir opened his eyes he felt calm.
He looked at his spots and felt brave.
Amir looked at Zola's big smile, he looked at the tree and it did not seem so large anymore.
With all his might, he Leaped onto the tree and climbed and climbed.
When he reached the top and looked down, he saw Zola smiling.
Amir said, "come on Zola it's not so bad up here". Zola jumped and climbed up to meet Amir.

It was getting late so Amir and Zola ran home.

When Amir's mother and father saw him, they were excited and gave
him a really big hug.
Amir's mom said, "Look at all your spots." His father said, "I am very
proud of you for facing so many fears today."
Amir's mom and dad asked how did you face your fears?
Amir said, "with Zola's help. Let me show you."

"Stand tall and proud and with your feet firm on the ground.
Close your eyes if you feel comfortable, and take a deep breath. In
through your nose filling your tummy and out though your nose
letting all the air out of your tummy.
I am calm,
I am confident, and
I am brave."
breath
confidant
calm
brave
CONFIDENT
CALM
BRAVE

He guides his mom and dad, and they follow along.
After they practiced, Amir's mom and dad, felt calm and focused.
Amir smiled, and looked at Zola and his spots; and said, "I am calm,
am confident, and I am brave."
spots   confidant   calm   brave
CONFIDENT   CALM   BRAVE

Guide to Mindfulness Practices and Yoga

Mantra A group of words or sounds repeated for meditation.

Amir Uses:
I am Calm
I am Confident
I am Brave

Mindfulness Developing a relationship with the body by paying attention to what is happening on the inside and outside of your body.

A goal of mindfulness is to calm down the business of your thoughts.

Practicing mindfulness is paying attention to breathing, focusing and being patient in the moment.

Ways to practice mindfulness: Close your eyes or focus on something in front of you that is not moving.
Pay attention to your breathing.

Breathing When practicing mindfulness breathing helps with creating a calm mind.
Zola teaches Amir to take a deep breath in through the nose filling the tummy and out through the nose letting all the air out of the tummy.

When things are scary taking the deep breaths will slow things down and bring forth calmness.

Yoga A series of movements to bring awareness to the body.

Amir Uses:

Brave Mountain Stand tall and proud with feet parallel and rooted into the earth.
Let the hands rest by the side with finger tips pointed to the earth.

Other Yoga Poses:

Proud Mountain Stand tall and proud with feet parallel and rooted into the earth. Lift the hands to the sky with fingers spread.

Leopard Cub Form the body like a leopard cub on all fours by coming to the earth on the hands and knees.
Place the palms flat on the earth and the knees apart.

Calm Leopard From Leopard Cub, touch the big toes together and spread the knees apart.
Stretch the arms forward and bring the hips back to meet the heels.
The forehead can rest on the earth.

Leopard Roar From Leopard Cub, Exhale and round the spine to the sky. Inhale move the spine in the opposite direction tummy towards the earth, facing forward and roar.
Move the spine up and down with your breath.

Baby Cub Lie on the back. Bring both of the knees towards the chest over the hips.
Grab the inner or outer soles of the feet with the knees to the outer sides of the torso.
Ground the bottom to the earth, creating a curve in the lower back.

Small Mountain Exhale and fold forward from the hips letting the fingertips touch the earth. Let the hips line up with your ankles.

Rising Mountain Fold halfway placing the hands on the kneecaps. Keep the knees soft, facing forward.

Leopard Lunge Place the fingertips in line with the toes. Center the knee over the heel.
Stepping one foot backwards.

Leopard Plank From Rising Mountain, step both feet back into the push up position.
Spread the fingers wide apart and with palms flat on the earth. Tuck the toes into the earth,
Focus the head forward and press the heels back.

Sneaky Cub Press the top of the feet into the earth. Place the hand outer shoulder width apart with the wrist directly below the elbows and forearms vertical with a bend. Lift the chest from the earth.

Down Cub From Leopard Cub, tuck the toes to the earth, press hands into the earth and raise the hips to the sky. Spread fingers and press into the earth Lift the inner shoulders.
Point the biceps in and squeeze the elbows straight.

Warrior Leopard From Mountain, step one foot back and bending the front knee, find balance and raise the hands to the sky.

Resting Cub Lie on the back with the legs stretched. Arms rested by the side palms facing up.

Hand Movements Glossary

Sun With a fist lightly make a circle on the middle of the back then draw rays from the circle.

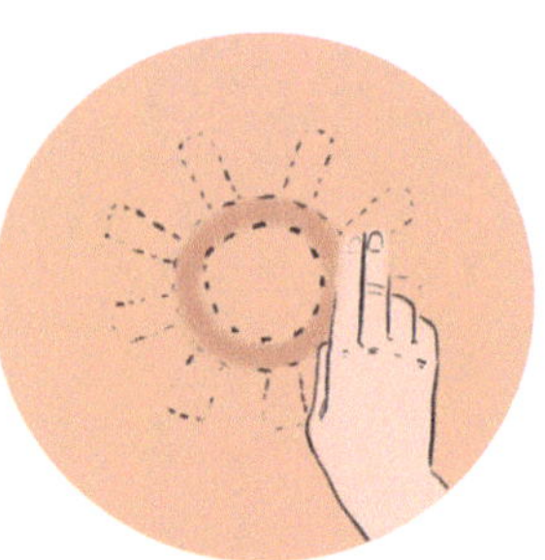

Cloud With two fingers flat on the back make an outline of a cloud.

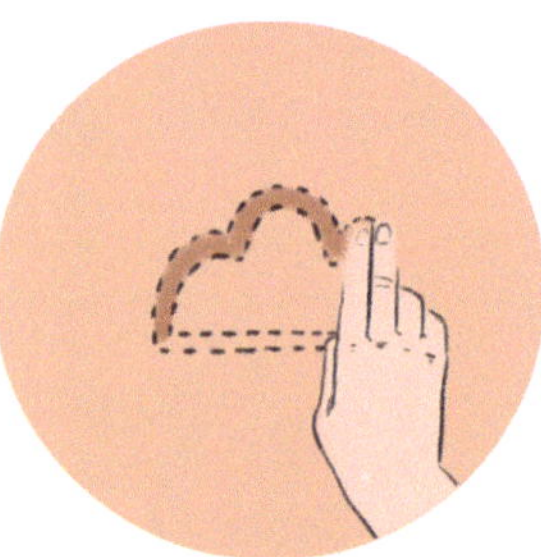

Waterfall With two fingers start at the top of the back making a half circle then let your hand flow down the back.

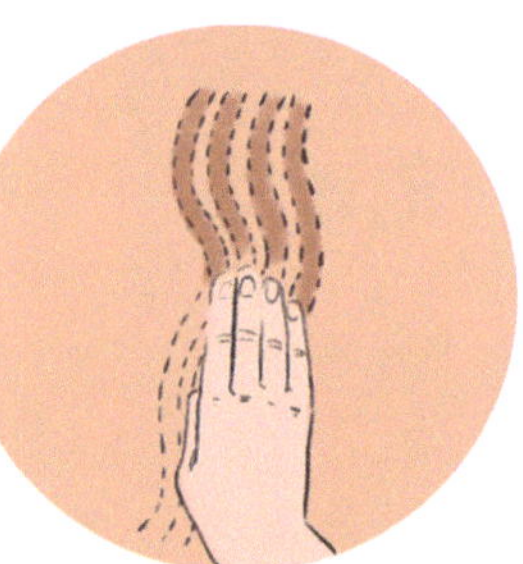

Lake With the two fingers in the middle of the back make up and down wave motions.

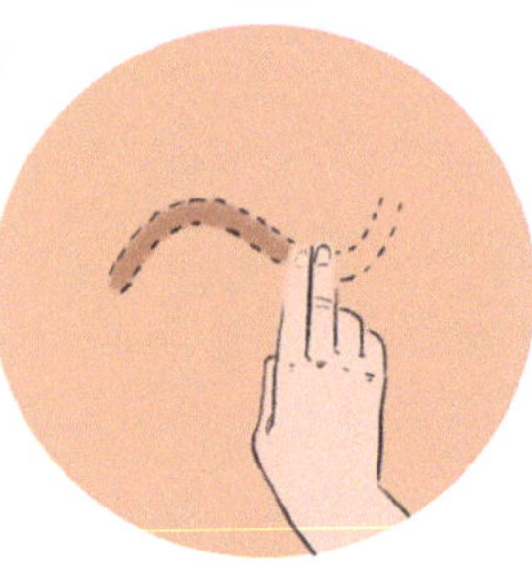

Run
Running Move fingers around the back in a running motion.

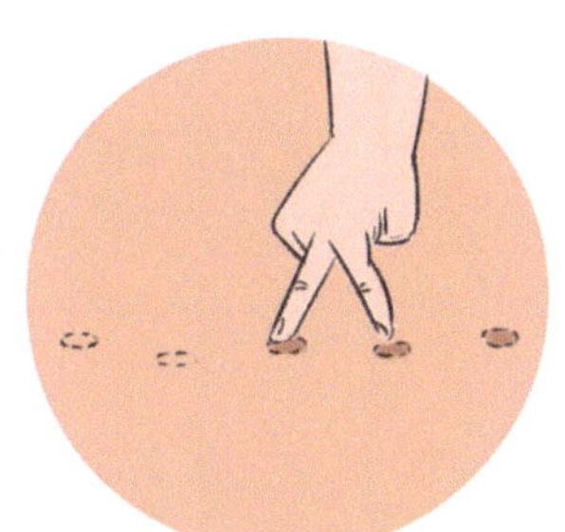

Jump
Leap With two fingers tap lightly across the back.

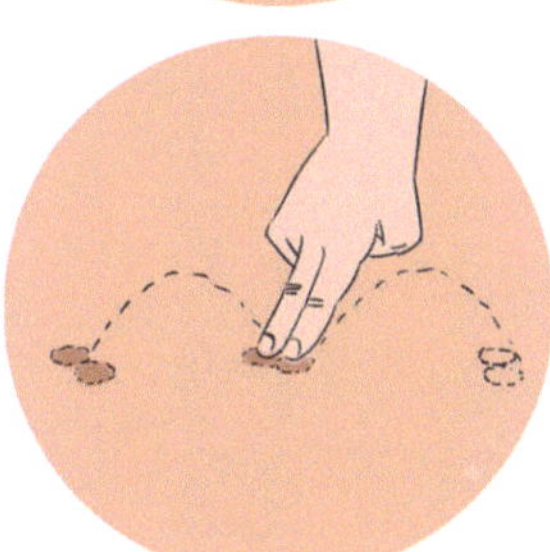

Happy Take fingers and draw a smiley face.

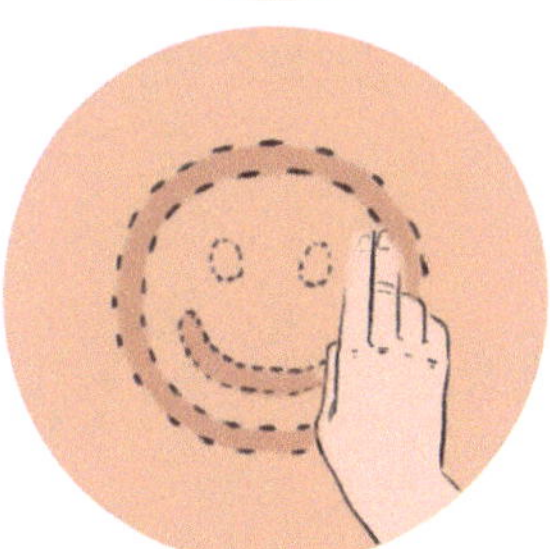

Spots Take two fingers and draw small circles on the middle of the back.

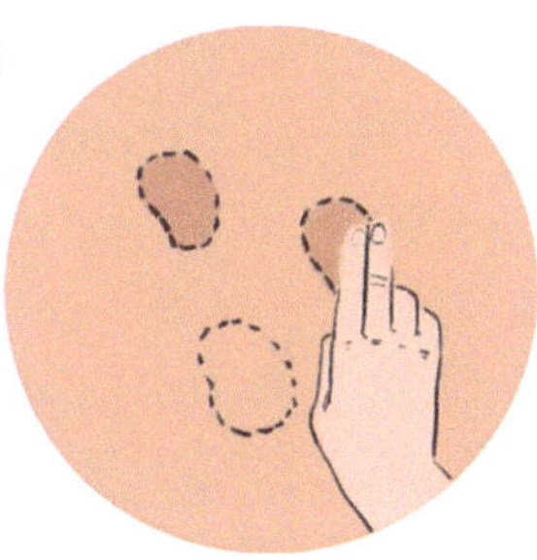

Tree Move fingers to create top of your tree then draw the foundation.

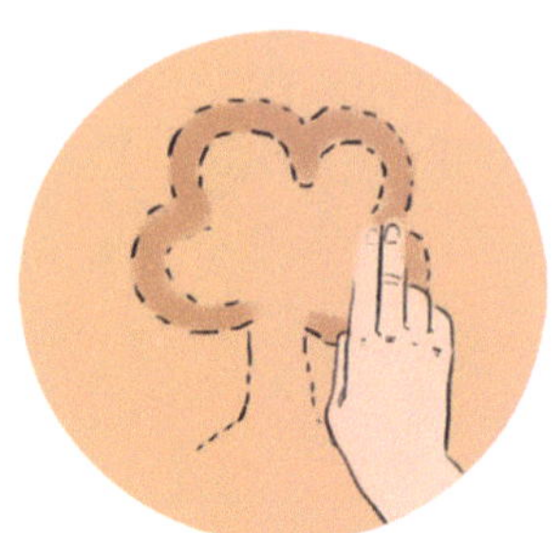

Heartbeat Using one finger from each hand start in the middle of the back and move both hands up then out then bringing fingers together at the bottom creating a heart. Then lightly tap inside of the heart.

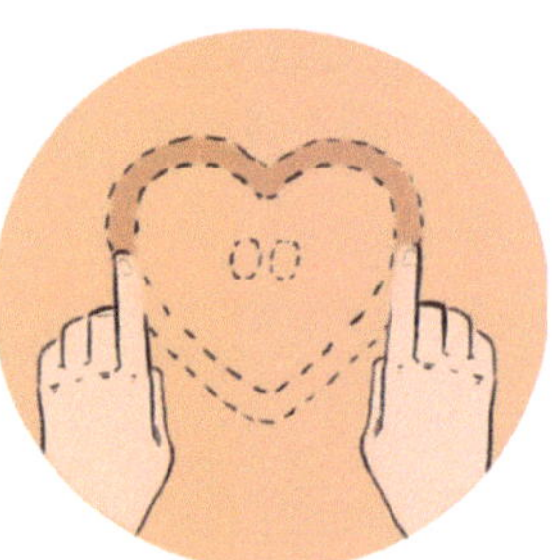

Heart Using one finger from each hand start in the middle of the back and move both hands up then out then bringing fingers together at the bottom creating a heart.

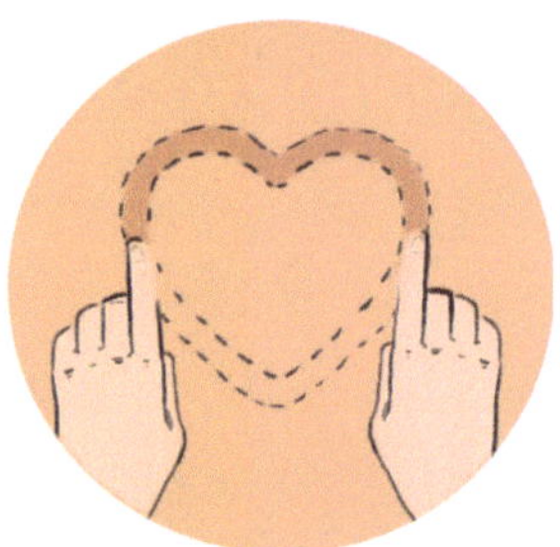

Breath Take a deep breath in through your nose and out through your mouth.

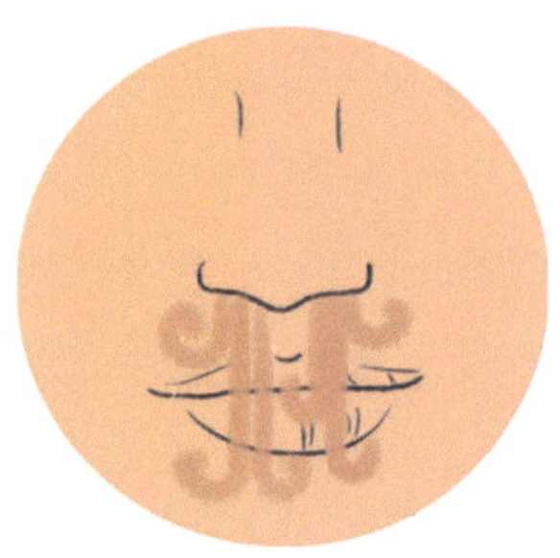

Climb Using finger pads of both hands, start at the bottom of the back and move toward the top.

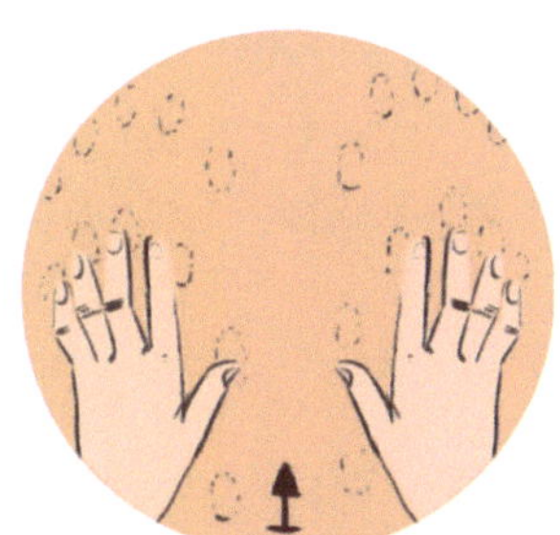

Hug Gentle hug. (you can replace with a handshake)

Grass With flat palms on the bottom of the back move fingers from side to side.

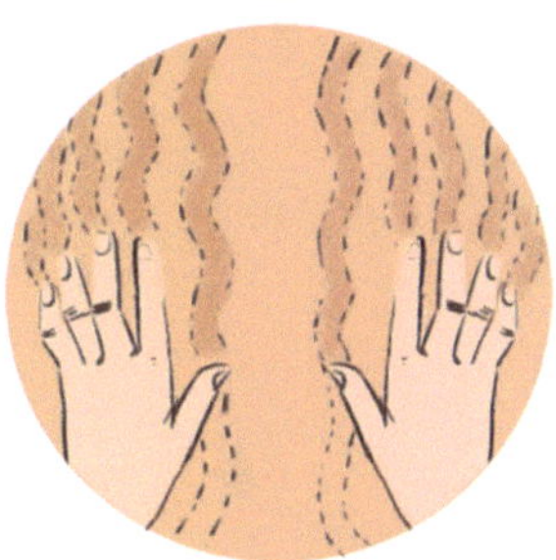

Brave
Calm
Trust
Safe
Confident

Words are spelled out on the back.

Amir's Brave Adventure

Like Amir you might have some fears.
Write them on Amir and when you face the fears color and make them brave spots!

It is ok to be a different color, Amir has earned his spots.
Color Amir to make him any color you would like.

Amir's Mantra

I am Calm!
I am Confidant!
I am Brave!

©Carmen Jimenez-Pride

Amir's Mantra Worksheet

On the lines provided write things that will make the sentence true.

I am Calm!

____

____

I am Confidant!

____

____

I am Brave!

____

____

Amir's friend Zola helped him during his adventure.
List people who help you to be calm, confident and brave.

Who help's be calm?

Who helps me be confident?

Who helps me be brave?

Draw a picture of you being brave.

Journal

Therapeutic Tips
for Mental Health Professionals, Parents, Teachers and other professionals working with children.

A key component to Kinesthetic Storytelling is touch, as a professional and parent we know that touch can be a form of attachment and comfort for some children and for others it can cause a great deal of anxiety.

As a professional you always want to make sure you ask for permission to touch. You can also guide the parent to ask the child for permission, this action build trust.

This story is interactive and can be expressed in various ways and maintain professional and safe guidelines. Therefore, as a professional you also want to follow your professional and ethical standards related to touch based activities with clients.

When working with the parent and child, a professional can demonstrate the touch base activities portions of the story on a stuff animal, while the parent is practicing the touch base activities on the child.

When working in a classroom or therapy room setting, the professional can adapt the touch base activities to meet the needs of the setting.

About the Author

Carmen K. Jimenez-Pride is a Master Level Social Worker, Substance Abuse Professional, Licensed Clinical Social Worker in North Carolina and Georgia. She is also a Licensed Independent Social Worker in South Carolina.

Carmen is a Registered Play Therapist Supervisor credentialed by the Association of Play Therapy. She earned a bachelor in Social Work with a certificate in Child Protective Services from Benedict College in 2004. She was accepted into the advance standing program at the University of South Carolina earning a Masters of Social Work in 2005 with a focus on communities and organizations.

Carmen has over 15 years of experience in the mental health field. In 2011, She created Outspoken Counseling and Consulting LLC.

In 2016 she became a Registered Yoga Teacher and in 2018 Carmen became a Registered Children Yoga Teacher. Carmen's yoga practice is trauma sensitive with a focus on children and play therapy.

Carmen is the founder of Play Therapy with Carmen Inc. an organization dedicated to educating the mental health community on play therapy and providing supervision, training and resources for licensed professionals.

Carmen's motto is "Together We Will Grow"